IS IT SUKKOT YET?

CHRIS BARASH

Pictures by
ALESSANDRA
PSACHAROPULO

ALBERT WHITMAN & COMPANY
CHICAGO, ILLINOIS

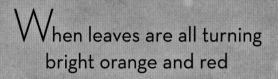

When leaves are all turning
bright orange and red

And it's time for the rakes to
come out of our shed...

Sukkot is on its way.

When squirrels and their friends
carry food that they've found

To store in the trees and
in dens underground...

Sukkot is on its way.

When we wear cozy pants and
warm shirts with long sleeves

To play with our friends in the cool autumn breeze...

Sukkot is on its way.

When the toolbox comes out

and the hammers bang hard
As we put up the hut that will stand in our yard...

Sukkot is on its way.

When Uncle Jake comes with his truck full of greens
For the roof of our sukkah—I know what that means...

Sukkot is on its way.

When big gourds and pumpkins are placed on the ground
And colorful streamers are hung all around...

Sukkot is on its way.

When our guests smell the *etrog's* bright lemony zest

And the *lulav* is waved north and south, east and west...

When the sunlight's grown dim as it quickly turns night

And we're snug in our sukkah
with moonbeams for light...

Sukkot is here!

Celebrate throughout the year with other books in this series!

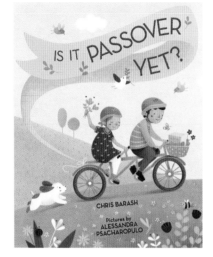

Is It Passover Yet?

Is It Hanukkah Yet?

Library of Congress Cataloging-in-Publication data
is on file with the publisher.

Text copyright © 2016 by Chris Barash
Pictures copyright © 2016 by Alessandra Psacharopulo
Published in 2016 by Albert Whitman & Company
ISBN 978-0-8075-3388-8

Printed in China
10 9 8 7 6 5 4 3 2 1 HH 24 23 22 21 20 19 18 17 16 15

Design by Jordan Kost

For more information about Albert Whitman & Company,
visit our web site at www.albertwhitman.com.